Gilles

Good For You, Mikey Mite!

Illustrations by Pierre-André Derome

Translated by Sarah Cummins

Formac Publishing Company Limited
Halifax, Nova Scotia 1996

Originally published as Le redoutable Marcus la puce.

Copyright © 1995 by les éditions de la courte échelle inc.

Translation copyright © 1996 by Formac Publishing Limited

Canadian Cataloguing in Publication Data

Gauthier, Gilles, 1943–

    [Redoutable Marcus la puce. English]

    Good for you, Mikey Mite

    (First novel series)

    Translation of: Le redoutable Marcus la puce.

ISBN 0-88780-370-9 (pbk.) — ISBN 0-88780-371-7 (bound)

I. Derome, Pierre André, 1952– II. Title. III. Title: Redoutable Marcus la puce. English. IV. Series.

PS8563.A858R4313   1996   jC843'.54   C96-950101-3
PZ7.G38Go 1996

Formac Publishing Limited
5502 Atlantic Street
Halifax, N.S. B3H 1G4

Printed and bound in Canada

Contents

1
Problems for Jenny

For the last couple of days, my parents have been on a single-minded crusade to get me away from Mikey Mite. I have tried to talk it over, to reason with them, but it's no good. They have their minds made up and nothing will make them change.

It all began when they heard tell of some of Mikey's exploits at school. There were incidents that I had miraculously managed to keep from their ears before this.

Mom started the attack by digging up an old story. She

wanted to know whether Mikey had really "borrowed" some carrots from the grocery store to feed to Attila, the guinea pig at our school.

Taken by surprise, I tried to defend Mikey as best I could.

I explained that Mikey didn't really feel he was stealing anything. He was just buying on credit and he intended to pay the storekeeper back later. I also pointed out that Mikey had grown up a lot since the carrots incident.

Mom didn't seem convinced. Neither did Dad. The interrogation continued the next day.

Dad said he was very surprised that I had never mentioned any of Mikey's run-ins with Mrs. Gesundheit, even though they were enough to make the principal switch Mikey to another class. Once again, I had trouble coming up with a good argument.

I tried to make the case that Mrs. Gesundheit's teaching methods just didn't work with Mikey. And I told them that Mikey is doing very well in school, now that he's in Miss Lum's class.

Dad and Mom looked at me very thoughtfully. I could tell that the investigation would come to a head very soon.

And I was right. That evening, Dad delivered the final blow. He said he thought it was very strange that I had never invited my friend Mikey to come over. He asked whether it was true that Mikey had recently broken his arm in a car accident.

I could see where my dad was heading, but I knew it was no use lying. So I told him it was true.

Then Mom started in. She asked if it was not also true that Mikey's father was drunk at the time of the accident.

I could tell that my friendship with Mikey Mite was seriously threatened. After a long silence, I said, very quietly, yes. Then I added, in a more confident tone, that Mikey's father had stopped drinking, that everything was fine now.

But this did not have the effect I was hoping for. Neither Mom nor Dad was willing to believe that everything was suddenly as perfect as I claimed. Dad sug-

gested that I should stay away
from Mikey for a while.

And that was that. There's
nothing I can say or do. My

parents are afraid of Mikey and his father. They're afraid for their little girl, and they want to protect her.

Even though they know nothing at all about the real Mikey Mite.

And even though my dad has been known to drink and drive himself ...

2
Break-up

Things are not going well for me, I must say. Not only do I have to stop seeing Mikey, now I have to give up Attila too! All because of my parents, who think that Mikey is the devil in person.

Mr. Chambers, the principal, called me down to his office this morning. He asked me to stop looking after Attila. He wants Mikey to take care of Attila by himself from now on.

Mr. Chambers explained that Attila is an important part of Mikey's life because Mikey doesn't have any friends. That is true, so I had no choice but to agree.

But I decided I would go talk to Mikey before I went home, just so he would understand exactly what had happened.

I hid in the back of the class-room where Attila is kept and waited for ten minutes. Every-one else was gone, and I was anxious for Mikey to show up.

I didn't want the janitor, Mr. Lotecki, to find me. Also I didn't want to get home from school too late or my parents would start to suspect something.

Finally! Mikey came in and walked over to Attila's cage. I called his name.

"Mikey! Hey, Mikey!"

Mikey jumped, but he recognized my voice. Looking surprised, he came over to my hiding place and I came out.

"Are you crazy, Jenny? You'll get caught!"

"I've got to talk to you. You deserve to know what's going on."

"I already know. Quick, get out of here before Mr. Lotecki finds you."

"Listen, Mikey. I have to explain. It's because of my parents that—"

"I know. I know all that already. Quick! Scram! Mr. Lotecki's coming!"

I ran back to my hiding place. But Mikey was lying. He was just trying to scare me, so I would leave.

The only sound was the pitter-patter of Attila's jogging feet.

"Mr. Lotecki is nowhere near, and you have to listen to me."

"I already know what you're going to say."

"My parents don't want me to hang around with you any more."

"Mr. Chambers told me."

"They think that you're a ..."

"... a thief. I know."

"And they heard that your father ..."

"... drinks."

When Mikey said that last word, he got all choked up. His eyes filled with tears.

Then he turned his back on me and went over to Attila's cage. I went after him, trying to comfort him.

"I told my parents that they were wrong, Mikey. I told them that your father has quit drinking and —"

Without turning around, Mikey yelled so loud that I was frozen in mid-step, "GET OUT OF HERE, JENNY!"

A terrible feeling swept through my body. For a second I couldn't speak. Then I tried to go on.

"I told my parents that your father—"

Mikey whirled around. He

had a mean look on his face that I had never seen before. He was beside himself.

"MY FATHER HAS STARTED DRINKING AGAIN! NOW, WILL YOU GET OUT OF HERE, JENNY!"

With this terrible news, and the terrifying look on Mikey's face, I couldn't find anything to say. I left the classroom and made my way home in tears.

My head felt empty, totally empty ... and my heart was horribly heavy.

3
Where is Mikey?

No one is getting any work done at school. No one is paying attention. We're all wondering what has happened to Mikey.

I haven't seen him since I left him in the classroom yesterday. His mother called our house to see if he was there. The police came and questioned me. I told them what I knew.

Overhearing them talking with my parents, I learned a few things. Mikey's father was drinking again yesterday. That's probably why Mikey ran away. They found his school bag in his bedroom.

I don't know what to think. Sometimes I blame myself and I feel guilty. I tell myself that I should have done something when Mikey told me his father had started drinking again.

Other times I tell myself that it wouldn't have made any difference anyway. Mikey's father would still have gotten drunk. Mikey would still have run away.

What worries me the most is Mikey's disappearance. When I think about it, I get scared. If I close my eyes for just two seconds, I imagine the very worst.

I can see Mikey on a bridge, staring down at the churning waters below. I see him trudging along the highway, buffeted by enormous trucks hurtling along at top speed.

I know it's stupid. It's only in my imagination and I should stop thinking about things like that. But when I remember Mikey yelling at me to leave,

when I see his face, I think to myself ... that anything could have happened, even the worst.

Mikey is so alone. He must feel so powerless to do anything to help his father.

Why can't my parents tell the difference between a good-for-nothing and a kid who is super unhappy?

4
Help me, Attila!

Mr. Chambers asked me to take care of Attila today, since Mikey isn't around. Of course, I said yes right away.

When I'm with Attila, I feel that I'm with Mikey too, in a way.

So here I am with the only friend Mikey has left. But one thing bothers me. Attila does not seem the least bit disturbed by the disappearance of his chief caregiver. He even seems strangely cheerful.

He has not stopped eating since I came in. Whenever he

pauses for a second, he gives me a sidelong look, as if he were enjoying a good joke.

I do not really appreciate him having so much fun when we don't know if Mikey is still al—

I feel like picking Attila up by the scruff of the neck and giving him a piece of my mind, telling him that he's an ungrateful, stupid ball of fur. I could just ...

It's funny. It seems as if Attila has read my mind. It looks like he just shook his head to say no. It's as if he's trying to get me to figure something out.

I know! I get it! I know why Attila doesn't seem concerned. It's because he knows Mikey is all right. He knows because Mikey told him.

Attila was the last one to see

Mikey after I left. I'm sure that Mikey confided in him.

Mikey is always talking to Attila when he takes care of him. I know he spoke to him before he left the school. I even have a pretty good idea of what he said.

As I look into Attila's eyes, I can almost hear Mikey's voice. I can't really hear it, that's for sure. I'm not crazy; I know that guinea pigs can't talk. But I hear it in my head.

When Attila has finished his feast, he carefully licks his paws clean. Then he looks straight at me, and his two bright brown beady eyes tell me what Mikey said to him.

"You know, Attila, I didn't yell at Jenny because I was mad

at her. It was because I was so sad, and I didn't want to make her feel worse than she already did. My father has started drinking again, Attila. And even though you and Jenny are my best friends, there's nothing you can do for him. So I decided that I have to do something. If I disappear for a while, maybe my dad will get a grip on himself ... Maybe he'll be afraid of losing me, and he'll quit drinking for good ... If he really cares about me ..."

"So that's what Mikey said, eh, Attila? And that's why you don't seem worried. You know that Mikey is alive and he'll be coming back soon. That's why you're so cheerful, right, Attila?"

Please tell me that's what he said ...

5
Mikey's misery

"Don't come any closer, or I'll throw it in your face."

"Calm down, Mikey. Be reasonable."

"I mean it, Mr. Lotecki. Take one more step and I'll throw this bottle right in your face."

"All right, Mikey. OK. I'll stay here. I won't move."

I can't believe my ears. Mr. Lotecki has just found Mikey. He was hiding in the room where the gym equipment is kept.

I was just finishing cleaning up Attila's cage, when I suddenly heard ...

"Stay back!"

It was Mikey's voice.

I ran joyfully to the door, but then I stopped short.

Mikey is standing on a pile of gym mats. There are beer bottles strewn all around him. He is holding one in his hand. He's swaying and has trouble talking. It's obvious he has been drinking.

Mr. Lotecki is a few metres away. He doesn't dare come closer since Mikey threatened him with the bottle. He is trying to calm Mikey down.

Neither one of them has seen me. I think I'll just stay out of sight for the time being, so that Mr. Lotecki can reason with Mikey.

"You don't need to be afraid, Mikey. No one is going to pun-

ish you for what you've done.
Everyone has been looking for
you, and they're very worried."

"Oh yeah! Sure! You can bet

that everyone cares a lot about what happens to *me*!"

"It's true, Mikey. Your parents, your friends, everyone ..."

"Yeah, I'll just bet my dad is looking for me. He can't even stand up. He's probably looking for me in the bottom of a bottle."

"Your mother is sick with worry, Mikey. We have to tell her, let her know that—"

"I told her it wouldn't last. I knew he would start drinking again. Mom's too kind. She just listens to all his promises, and she believes him!"

"Your father stopped drinking for three months, Mikey. Then he fell off the wagon. You shouldn't—"

"He's fallen off the wagon about twenty thousand times.

He has to stop once and for all. He has to stay on the wagon."

Mikey is staggering around on the mats. He looks pale and his hair is tousled. He must not have slept at all last night.

"It's not easy to stop drinking for good, you know, Mikey."

"Do you think it's easy living with a father like him? What a ... Sometimes I just feel like ..."

Mikey's face looks hard. His hand is shaking and his eyes are frightening.

"Calm down, Mikey. You've got to calm down. I'm going to speak to your mother and to the principal."

"I don't want to see them. I don't want to see anyone. Do you hear me? Nobody. I want everybody to just leave me alone. I'm tired ..."

Mikey can't hold on any longer. He lowers the hand that is holding the bottle. Huge tears are streaming down his face.

Mr. Lotecki steps forward.

"You can rest now, Mikey. I'll help you. Just like I did when you had troubles with Steve and his gang."

"The only difference is that my father is not Steve. You can't punish him by making him clean out Attila's cage. My father's not a kid."

"I know your father better than you think."

"You've never even met my father. He's never come to the school. You're just saying that to make me believe you. All you want is for me to go back home and stop bothering everybody."

"No, Mikey. When I said I would help you, I meant it."

"And how can you help me any better than the others?"

"Because ... because I used to have the same problem as your father. And I was able to overcome it."

Mikey stands stock still. He stops talking and stares at Mr. Lotecki in disbelief.

Mr. Lotecki smiles and nods his head.

"That's right. I used to drink too, Mikey. Maybe even more than your father. And since I was able to stop, I know that other people can stop too. Trust me, Mikey. I can help your father."

Mikey closes his eyes. He drops his bottle. It falls to the

floor. Mikey bursts into sobs.

Mr. Lotecki wraps his enormous arms around him and holds him close.

A mite, held in the arms of a giant ...

6
The promise

I haven't seen Mikey Mite for three days. He's stayed home from school since the day Mr. Lotecki found him. But he'll be coming back today. Mr. Lotecki told me.

Mr. Lotecki is amazing! He took care of everything on the day he found Mikey.

He phoned Mikey's mother to tell her that her son was fine. He also called Mr. Chambers, who hurried over to the school. Together they took Mikey home.

But before calling the principal, Mr. Lotecki made me promise something. He asked me not to tell anyone what I had seen and heard. He wants to keep it between the three of us—just Mikey, him, and me. I agreed one hundred per cent, and I promised to keep the secret.

I could tell that Mikey felt relieved. So did I. I wouldn't like my parents to know what Mikey had done, given their present opinion of him.

Mikey's parents seemed to have taken it all very well. Mr. Lotecki told me that Mikey's mother wept for joy when her son came home, and she held him in her arms for a long, long time.

His father was embarrassed. He hardly dared look at Mikey. Finally he muttered that he understood why Mikey had done what he did and that he was very sorry.

I can hardly wait until school is over so I can talk to Mikey.

My parents have forbidden me to see him, but I'm going to anyway.

It must be very hard for Mikey to face the whole school after what he did. He needs to know that someone still loves him.

His best friend will be there.

7
Two more A's

I don't know whether it's an act or not, but Mikey seems to be in very good spirits. He whistles constantly while combing Attila's coat, having a lot of fun with his famous toothbrush turned fur-brush. I must admit I have trouble keeping up with him.

I tried to get him to talk to me, but no luck. He told me that first he had to look after Attila, who must have missed him. He even wondered aloud how well I had been taking care of "his" Peruvian guinea pig while he was away.

From his laughing tone, I could tell he was only joking.

Attila, at any rate, is delighted to have Mikey back. He coos and babbles and chortles. If he wasn't so fat, I bet he would fly around in his cage.

Mikey is cooing and babbling too. He imitates all of Attila's little songs. I wish I knew what's behind this comic opera.

When he has finally finished grooming his prize tenor, Mikey announces that we are both going to the park. He doesn't listen when I remind him that I have to go straight home from school.

Now, Mikey is pumping higher and higher on the swing next to mine. I think he would like to fly away into the sky too.

"So, Mikey, will you tell me

what's going on? My parents are going to flip out. I can't stay here forever."

Mikey smiles and stretches his toes toward the clouds.

"Okay, I'll tell you what's going on. I have two more A's."

Mikey made the same joke about two A's when his dad joined Alcoholics Anonymous. Probably his dad is going back to AA.

"Has your father decided to get help again?"

"Better than that!"

I don't know what he is talking about, and I am beginning to get impatient to leave.

"Come on, Mikey! Cough it up! Otherwise I'll have to leave without finding out what you're talking about."

Mikey gives another tremendous pump, then he says proudly, "I have two more A's, thanks to Mr. Lotecki."

Seeing the question marks in my eyes, Mikey finally decides that the suspense has gone on long enough. "Mr. Lotecki has been in AA for ten years," he announces. "So he is going to be my dad's sponsor."

"What do you mean, his sponsor? Like an athlete's sponsor?"

Mikey makes a face.

"Of course not, you nut! Just someone who looks after you when you have a problem and other people don't know what to do."

"That's great, Mikey! I can't believe it. I can see why you're happy."

Mikey smiles from ear to ear and gives a last big push on his swing.

"I can't believe it either. This

time, Jenny, I believe it's really going to work. With Mr. Lotecki."

Crazy with joy, Mikey lets go of the chains on the swing and leaps into the air, his arms outstretched like the wings of a bird.

For a moment, it really looks like he is flying through the air. He shines in the sunlight like a seabird.

But then the seabird lands in a puddle. When Mikey gets up, his sweater is all covered with mud.

8
A wonderful mistake

Life is strange. Sometimes the best things come out of your mistakes.

I had no intention of telling my parents that Mr. Lotecki used to drink. That was supposed to be a secret for Mikey, Mr. Lotecki, and me. But I was so happy about Mikey that I told my parents about his father's sponsor. So they found out about everything.

The next morning they were sitting in Mr. Chambers' office. And that is when my big mistake turned into something incredibly lucky. Mr. Lotecki told me all about it.

My parents could not understand why they had not been informed earlier about Mikey and his family. They could not understand why the school would hire a former alcoholic as janitor, either.

First Mr. Chambers tried to get across to them his own point of view. But since it is hard to get my parents to change their minds, he soon ran out of arguments. That was when he had the brilliant idea of calling Mr. Lotecki in.

Mr. Lotecki is a man of few words. When he does speak, he says exactly what he means without beating around the bush.

My parents are used to listening to great intellectuals. Some of the people who come to our house for dinner can come up with sentences a yard long. But somehow Mr. Lotecki managed to convince them.

To me, it seems like a genuine miracle!

My parents have finally realized that it is possible for someone to quit drinking for good. They also seem to understand now that Mikey is not a little terror.

I don't know how Mr. Lotecki did it. I only know that he told them how he used to act when he was in school. He was a lot worse than Mikey. Since he was so big, he was a real terror. He was wild when he was young.

He was sent from one school to another. He got in trouble with the police and was even sent to a kind of prison.

Still, one day, he decided to change. And he did, with the help of a friend who also had overcome great problems.

Mr. Lotecki must have been convincing because my parents finally decided to give me a little breathing space. I now have permission to take care of Attila with Mikey.

My parents still don't want me playing with Mikey after school. But they've taken the first step. I have to give them time. Maybe, in the long run, they'll realize not everyone is the same.

Just because you do some

crazy things once doesn't mean you're a good-for-nothing forever.

You can also be a janitor and know how to fix more than just broken windows.

9
Ups and downs

Things are looking up these days for Mikey Mite. His father hasn't touched a drop for a month. He talked with Mikey about his drinking problem and explained that it was something he himself had to work through.

He also told him about his recent relapse.

And strange as it might seem, Mikey says that this time it was a problem with writing!

Mikey's father has worked in a factory for nearly thirty years. He applied for a better job but he didn't get it. He didn't get it because he doesn't know how to write very well.

He was so discouraged that he reacted in the usual way, by drinking. Until Mr. Lotecki stepped in.

When Mikey found this out, he decided to work very hard at writing himself, so his father would be proud of him.

He has fewer and fewer mistakes on his spelling tests, and Miss Lum even read one of his compositions aloud to the class. Mikey had written about a poor little guinea pig that became the Emperor of Peru.

All of his classmates were rolling on the floor with laughter. According to Mikey, Attila was very flattered to have been his inspiration.

So things are going very well these days. So well that my parents have decided to take another step. They've allowed me to have lunch with Mikey at a restaurant.

But there is one little matter that I did not dare mention to

them: there would be another guest.

Mikey insisted we take Attila with us. I tried to get him to change his mind, but he wouldn't. Now Mikey is sitting next to me at the counter, and Attila is tucked in his windbreaker.

So far, everything has been fine. The waitress has no idea there is a guinea pig sitting at the counter. From time to time Mikey sneaks a french fry to Attila, who gobbles it up.

However, Mikey has ordered chocolate ice cream for dessert. This has got me worried.

The waitress has just set an enormous dish of ice cream in front of Mikey. He smiles nervously. He's having trouble keeping his guinea pig still.

Attila squealed just as the waitress was turning away. Mikey tried to cover it up by whistling loudly. I think she thinks he's weird.

To calm Attila down, Mikey is trying to sneak him spoonfuls of ice cream. But it's not easy.

With every spoonful, Attila goes wild. He waves his paws all around, and a lot of the ice cream never reaches his mouth.

Mikey's windbreaker looks like a leopard skin, all spotted with chocolate. And dumb old Attila keeps on wiggling.

Now he's escaped from Mikey's hands. He's running along the counter towards our neighbour's glass. The poor man has no idea!

Oh no! Attila knocks the glass

over. The guy almost has a heart attack when he sees Attila.

Mikey apologizes to the waitress. He hurries back with his dripping guinea pig.

Despite his troubles, Mikey can't keep from laughing. He hands me Attila, who is now wearing a mustache of beer-foam.

"Another case for the AA!" says Mikey.

He always keeps me laughing!